JP
JUD

For Willow,
with special thanks to Reka Simonsen and Sonia Chaghatzbanian

ATHENEUM BOOKS FOR YOUNG READERS • An imprint of Simon & Schuster Children's Publishing Division • 1230 Avenue of the Americas, New York, New York 10020 • © 2022 by Lita Judge • Book design by Sonia Chaghatzbanian © 2022 by Simon & Schuster, Inc. • All rights reserved, including the right of reproduction in whole or in part in any form. • ATHENEUM BOOKS FOR YOUNG READERS is a registered trademark of Simon & Schuster, Inc. Atheneum logo is a trademark of Simon & Schuster, Inc. • For information about special discounts for bulk purchases, please contact Simon & Schuster Special Sales at 1-866-506-1949 or business@simonandschuster.com. • The Simon & Schuster Speakers Bureau can bring authors to your live event. For more information or to book an event, contact the Simon & Schuster Speakers Bureau at 1-866-248-3049 or visit our website at www.simonspeakers.com. • The text for this book was set in Garamond. • The illustrations for this book were rendered in watercolor and digitally edited. • Manufactured in China • 0222 SCP • First Edition • 2 4 6 8 10 9 7 5 3 1 • Library of Congress Cataloging-in-Publication Data • Names: Judge, Lita, author, illustrator. • Title: Something beautiful / Lita Judge. • Description: First edition. | New York : Atheneum Books for Young Readers, 2022. | Audience: Ages 4 to 8. | Summary: "Mouse, Elephant, and Giraffe have so much in common. They like the same games. They eat the same snacks. They need no one else! Or do they? Perhaps there's something beautiful in making new friends"—Provided by publisher. • Identifiers: LCCN 2021007392 | ISBN 9781534485136 (hardcover) | ISBN 9781534485143 (ebook) • Subjects: CYAC: Friendship—Fiction. | Individuality—Fiction. | Jungle animals—Fiction. • Classification: LCC PZ7.J894 So 2022 | DDC [E]—dc23 • LC record available at https://lccn.loc.gov/2021007392

Something Beautiful

lita judge

atheneum

Atheneum Books for Young Readers
New York London Toronto Sydney New Delhi

Ball was Mouse's favorite,
and with it, he played alone.

Then one day Elephant asked to play.

Mouse and Elephant shared Ball,

until . . .

they met Giraffe.

"Eight, nine, ten—ready or not, here I come."

Mouse, Elephant, and Giraffe had so much in common. They liked the same games.

They ate the same snacks. They needed no one else.

But then Porcupine
said, "Hi!"

At first, Mouse, Elephant, and Giraffe weren't sure about someone new.

After all, he wasn't good at their games,

and he ate strange snacks.

But they never knew that they
loved to climb trees until
Porcupine taught them how.

Mouse, Elephant, Giraffe, and Porcupine
needed no one else, but then . . .

Warthog stopped by.

Warthog had a heart full of sunshine
and a head full of dreams.

Together, they discovered that flowers
were magic wands in disguise

and that ears can be
turned into wings.

Mouse, Elephant, Giraffe, Porcupine, and Warthog
needed no one else,

but then . . .

they tripped over Lion's tail.

"Sorry!"

Lion looked lonely.

The friends invited him to play.

But he only wanted to sit.
Mouse, Elephant, Giraffe, Porcupine, and Warthog
stopped playing and sat with him.

At first, it seemed very dull to be Lion's friend, but then . . .

he showed them that if you are
patient and sit quietly . . .

something beautiful may unfold.

Together, Mouse, Elephant, Giraffe, Porcupine,
Warthog, and Lion explored the world . . .

and found that each of them,
in their own unique way, was also . . .

something beautiful.